CAMILA
THE DANCING STAR

written by *ALICIA SALAZAR*

illustrated by *THAIS DAMIÃO*

PICTURE WINDOW BOOKS
a capstone imprint

Published by Picture Window Books, an imprint of Capstone
1710 Roe Crest Drive, North Mankato, Minnesota 56003
capstonepub.com

Library of Congress Cataloging-in-Publication Data
Names: Salazar, Alicia, 1973- author. | Damião, Thais, illustrator.
Title: Camila the dancing star / by Alicia Salazar ; illustrated by Thais Damião.
Description: North Mankato, Minnesota : Picture Window Books, an imprint of
Capstone, [2022] | Series: Camila the star | Audience: Ages 5-7. | Audience:
Grades K-1. | Summary: At dance camp, Camila teams up with new friends
Lulu and Raisa, and they enter a dance competition. But when Camila injures
her ankle, it looks like they are out of the contest, until Raisa suggests they
perform a sitting dance from India.
Identifiers: LCCN 2021019161 (print) | LCCN 2021019162 (ebook) |
ISBN 9781663958693 (hardcover) | ISBN 9781666331615 (paperback) |
ISBN 9781666331622 (pdf)
Subjects: LCSH: Hispanic American girls—Juvenile fiction. | Dance—Juvenile
fiction. | Contests—Juvenile fiction. | Friendship—Juvenile fiction. | CYAC:
Dance—Fiction. | Contests—Fiction. | Friendship—Fiction. | Hispanic
Americans—Fiction.
Classification: LCC PZ7.1.S2483 Cah 2022 (print) | LCC PZ7.1.S2483 (ebook) |
DDC 813.6 [E]—dc23
LC record available at https://lccn.loc.gov/2021019161
LC ebook record available at https://lccn.loc.gov/2021019162

Designer: Hilary Wacholz

Printed and bound in the USA. PO4608

TABLE OF CONTENTS

Meet Camila and Her Family

Papá

Mamá

Ana, age 14

Andres, age 10

Camila, age 7

Spanish Glossary

bailarina (bah-ee-lah-REE-nah)—dancer

un equipo (oon eh-KEE-poh)—a team

Las Estrellas (lahs eh-STREH-yahs)—The Stars

música (MOO-see-kah)—music

la perfección (lah per-fek-SYOHN)—perfection

Chapter 1

A WEEK AT DANCE CAMP

It was Camila's first day at dance camp.

The camp counselor, Mrs. Lennox, made an announcement. It was **música** to Camila's ears.

"The summer dance competition will be held at the end of the week," boomed Mrs. Lennox.

"The sign-up sheet is hanging
on my office door," she added.
"The winner gets a spot in the
Los Angeles Dance Showcase
next year!"

"We would be stars!" she told Raisa and Lulu, her new friends.

"How?" asked Lulu.

"By winning and being in the showcase," said Camila.

"Alina Henris is one of the judges," said Raisa, bouncing.

"She is the greatest **bailarina** in the world!" Camila clapped. "I have to meet her!"

"Can all three of us win?" asked Lulu.

"If we are **un equipo**, we can," said Camila.

Camila, Lulu, and Raisa signed up as a team named **Las Estrellas**. They got right to work on their dance.

"Five, six, seven, eight."
Camila counted off the **música**.

The three of them stepped,
turned, and twirled together.
At first, they missed a step
or two.

"Practice makes **la
perfección**," said Camila.

They practiced and practiced.
Their only breaks were to eat
and rest.

Chapter 2

A NEW DANCE

On the third day, Camila was running to dance class when she fell and twisted her ankle.

Mrs. Lennox took her straight to the clinic.

"You won't be able to walk
on that foot for a few weeks, let
alone dance!" said the nurse. She
handed Camila a pair of crutches.

"If I'm not in the competition,
I won't be a star. And I won't
meet Alina Henris!" said Camila.
Tears welled up in her eyes.

"I'm sorry," Camila said to Lulu and Raisa. "I can't be on the team."

"Wait," said Raisa. "In India, we have a sitting dance that you dance sitting on the floor. I'll show you."

Raisa sat on the floor and swayed to a silent rhythm.

"I don't want to ruin the plans," said Camila. "You don't have to change the dance for me."

"We are **Las Estrellas**," said Raisa.

"We are a team," said Lulu. "We can't dance without you."

Camila, Lulu, and Raisa agreed to perform the sitting dance.

They kept practicing every day.

They turned and swayed to the music until every move was perfect.

Chapter 3

BRIGHT, SHINY STARS

Finally, it was the night of the competition. Lulu and Raisa helped Camila sit on the floor in the middle of the stage. They sat down on either side of her.

The music started and so did
they. They turned and swayed
until the music ended.

Las Estrellas took a bow.
Then they watched the other
teams perform.

They were excited and nervous to watch. It wasn't that they wanted the other teams to lose. It was just that they wanted **Las Estrellas** to win.

First were the Rocket Girls. They slid, skipped, and rolled.

Camila's heart was in her mouth. "They are really good," she thought.

Next were the Fireballs. They jumped, flipped, and stomped.

Camila bit her lip. "It's going to be close," she thought.

One by one, the rest of the teams danced.

"All of the teams were really good," said Camila. Lulu and Raisa agreed.

The three friends held hands and listened to the results.

"The winner of the summer dance competition is . . ." announced Mrs. Lennox. ". . . the Rocket Girls!"

Camila's heart fell. "We can't be stars since we didn't win," she said.

"You guys did great out there," said a woman's voice.

They turned. It was Alina Henris. She was walking on crutches.

"I sprained my ankle too," she said. "I lost my spot in the show this summer."

"But you are a star," said Camila.

"Being a star is about working hard," said Alina. "All three of you were stars tonight!"

"As bright and shiny as you?" asked Camila.

"As bright and shiny as the sun!" said Alina.

Just Dance with Balloons!

Dancing is a great way to get exercise and let loose, either with friends or all by yourself! Put on music, and bust out your moves to feel the groove. For extra fun, try this dancing game.

WHAT YOU NEED
- a balloon for each dancer
- a radio, phone, or another device that plays music

WHAT YOU DO
1. Give each dancer a different color balloon and turn on some upbeat music.
2. Start dancing and juggling the balloons.
3. The balloons cannot be held, and they cannot fall down. Each dancer must keep their colored balloon up in the air by tapping it up as needed. If a balloon falls to the ground, the dancer is out.
4. The dancer who dances with their balloon the longest wins!

Glossary

announcement (uh-NAUNTS-muhnt)— information that is shared out loud or in a note

camp counselor (KAMP KOUN-suh-lur)—a person who works with children and leads activities at a camp

clinic (KLI-nik)—a place where people go to receive medical care

competition (kahm-puh-TI-shuhn)—a contest

crutch (KRUHCH)—a long wooden or metal stick with a padded top; people with leg injuries often uses crutches to help them walk

showcase (SHOH-kayss)—a special event where performers share their acts

Think About the Story

1. Explain why Camila wants to win the dance competition. When her team signs up, do you think she is more interested in the fun of dancing or the fun of winning? Does that change throughout the story?

2. How did Camila feel when she hurt her ankle? What words and picture clues tell you this?

3. On page 21, it says, "Camila's heart was in her mouth" as she watched another team dance. What does that mean?

4. Alina says, "Being a star is about working hard." What is something that you are a star at?

About the Author

Alicia Salazar is a Mexican American children's book author who has written for blogs, magazines, and educational publishers. She was also once an elementary school teacher and a marine biologist. She currently lives in the suburbs of Houston, Texas, but is a city girl at heart. When Alicia is not dreaming up new adventures to experience, she is turning her adventures into stories for kids.

About the Illustrator

Thais Damião is a Brazilian illustrator and graphic designer. Born and raised in a small city in Rio de Janeiro State, Brazil, she spent her childhood playing with her brother and cousins and drawing all the time. Her illustrations are dedicated to children and inspired by nature and friendship. Thais currently lives in California.